BY ANDRIA WARMFLASH ROSENBAUM

ILLUSTRATED BY EDWIN FOTHERINGHAM

SCHOLASTIC PRESS | NEW YORK

Big Ter, TLe STer

HEY, WAIT FOR ME!

Lucy thought
her little sister,

Mia,
was a
monster.

She followed Lucy

everywhere.

She borrowed Lucy's things without asking.

She didn't sit still at Spa La Lucy.

And sometimes
she stole Lucy's spotlight.

When Mia surprised Lucy
with a new *pet*, Lucy cried,

So Mia left.

And Lucy was alone
at last!

No one trailed her like a tail.

Her stuff stayed tidy.

Her toothbrush — paint-free.

But after a while, it felt quiet.

Very quiet.

TOO QUIET.

No one followed Lucy's lead.

And a show starring one
wasn't much fun.

So Lucy went
to find Mia.
She searched their usual hideouts.
She looked high and low.

But Mia was **nowhere.**

Then she spotted a strange door
drawn on Mia's wall.
Lucy touched it . . . and it

OPENED!

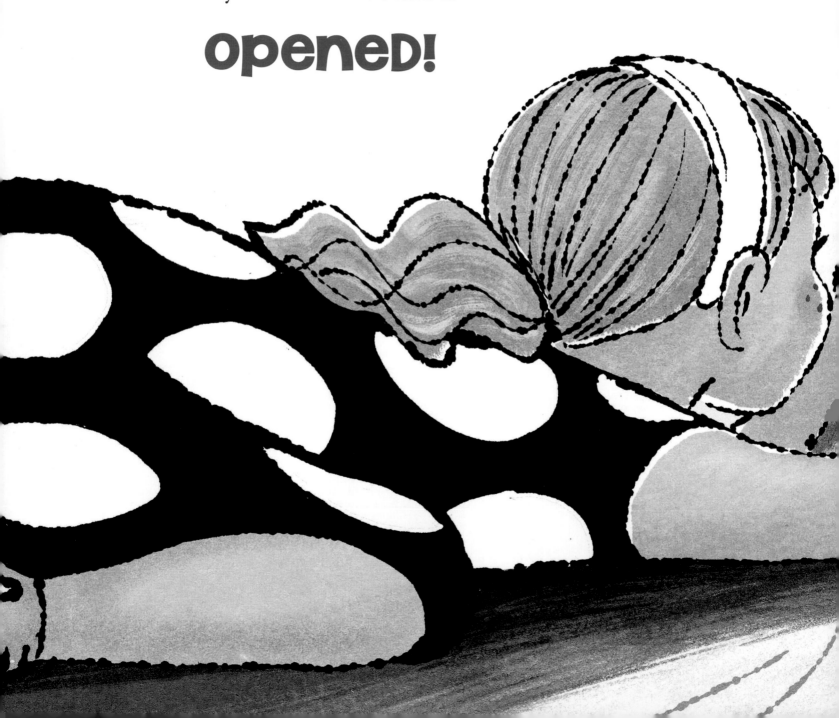

She timidly peeked inside.

There was Mia, surrounded by . . .

MONSTERS!

"Who are you?" hissed a slimy monster.

"I'm Lucy, Mia's s-sister," she stuttered.

"Sister? Shmister!" growled a grimy monster. "You're not like Mia!"

"Mia prances in puddles," snorted a scaly monster.

"She paints with pudding," sang a fangy monster.
"She's rule-free and ready to romp," bellowed
a furry monster.
"Monster Mia is our queen!" they hollered.
"We're keeping her forever!"

FOREVER?

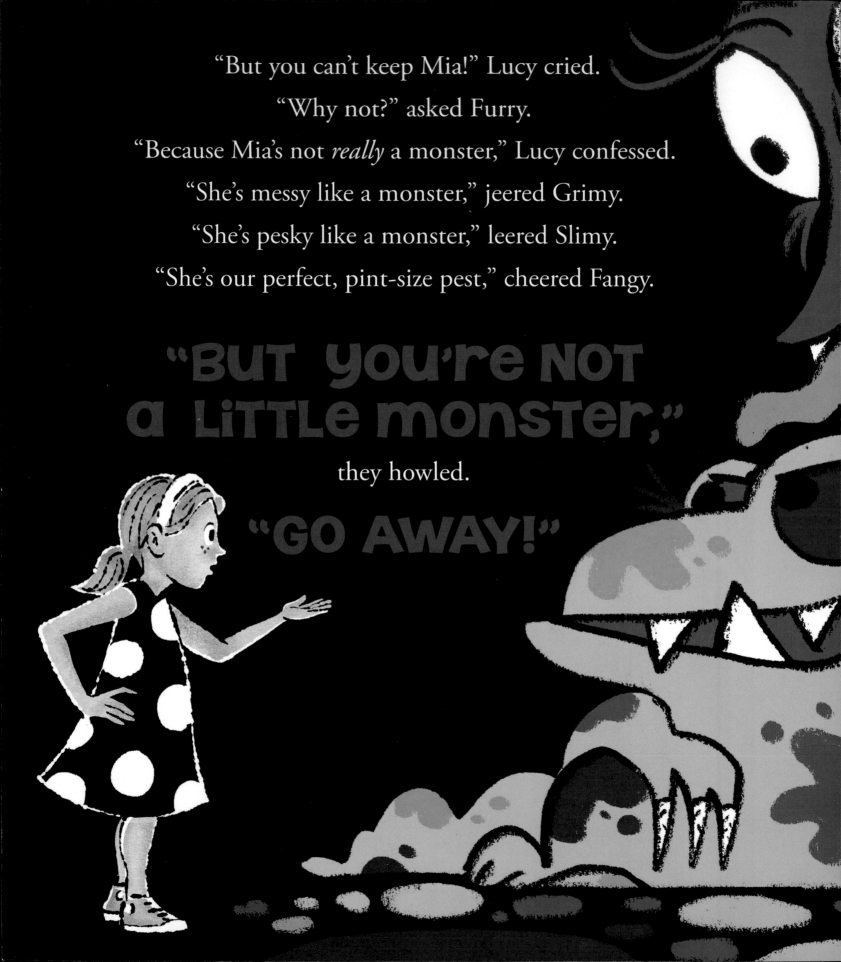

"But you can't keep Mia!" Lucy cried.

"Why not?" asked Furry.

"Because Mia's not *really* a monster," Lucy confessed.

"She's messy like a monster," jeered Grimy.

"She's pesky like a monster," leered Slimy.

"She's our perfect, pint-size pest," cheered Fangy.

"BUT YOU'RE NOT
A LITTLE MONSTER,"

they howled.

"GO AWAY!"

Lucy's heart hammered.

What had she done?

Her head yammered.

No more Mia?

That made Lucy mad.

very maD.

Mad enough . . . to find just what she needed.

Her **INNER** monster!

"GIVE
ME
BACK
MY
SISTER!"

LUCY ROARED.

The monsters shivered.
The monsters quivered.

"EEEEE

EEEKKKKK!! "

they shrieked. "You are *much* too monstrous!"
Then they hurried-scurried all the way home.

Lucy hugged her sister
with all her might.
"I missed you, Mia,"
she said.
"Mud pies or puddles?"

"BOTH!"

Sometimes
Lucy and Mia
were
little
monsters.

Sometimes
they were
not.

But they were always . . . **SISTERS.**

For Valerie . . . always,
and Penny, Queen of Hearts —AWR

For my family —EF

All rights reserved. Published by Scholastic Press, an imprint of Scholastic Inc., *Publishers since 1920.*
SCHOLASTIC, SCHOLASTIC PRESS, and associated logos are trademarks and/or registered trademarks of Scholastic Inc.

LIBRARY OF CONGRESS CATALOGING-IN-PUBLICATION DATA AVAILABLE

ISBN 978-0-545-83192-5

10 9 8 7 6 5 4 3 2 1   17 18 19 20 21

Printed in China   38

First edition, September 2017

The text type was set in Adobe Garamond Pro.
The display type was set in KG The Last Time.
The illustrations were done in digital media.

Book design by Marijka Kostiw